Prince
What-a-Mess

Frank Muir
Illustrated by Joseph Wright

First published 1979 by Ernest Benn Limited.
25 New Street Square, London EC4A 3JA.
& Sovereign Way, Tonbridge, Kent TN9 1RW.
© Frank Muir Limited. 1979.
Illustrations © Joseph Wright 1979.
Printed in England by W.S. Cowell Ltd. Ipswich

ISBN 0 510-00063-0.

Ernest Benn
LONDON & TONBRIDGE

The sun shone hotly, birds chirruped, small creatures played games in the long grass, but What-a-Mess paid no attention. He was busy having a Big Think.
He was having it on top of a car – What-a-Mess loved being high up when he was thinking.

The trouble was that his Big Think was not going too well. He kept dozing off and forgetting what he was supposed to be thinking about. He had brought a bag of walnuts up with him in case he collapsed from hunger during his Think, and he bit into one of these. The walnut rolled off the car roof. He tried to bite another but that rolled off, too.

He jumped to his feet and did a little dance to cheer himself up. With a loud "TUNK!" the car roof buckled under his weight. This made a nice comfortable dent into which What-a-Mess settled with his walnuts, which now rolled inwards when he dropped them.

Happy again, he resumed his Big Think.

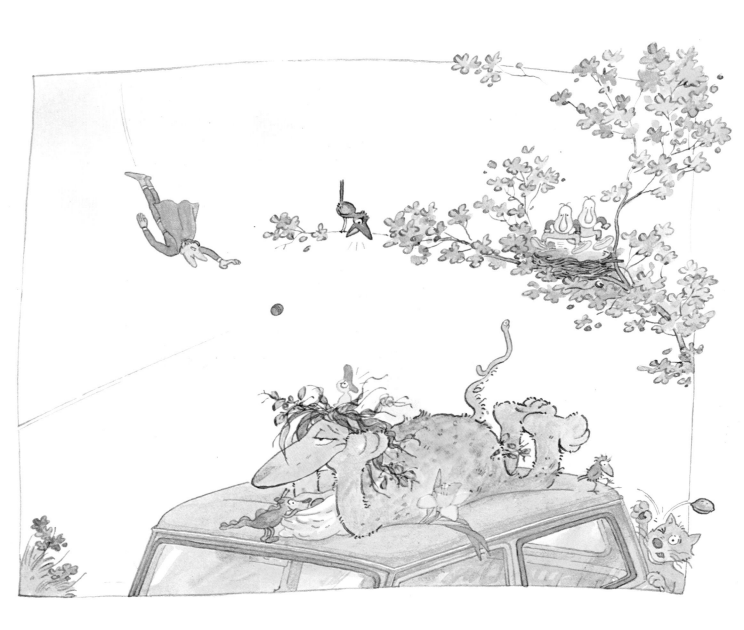

"I am not a puppy any more," he said to himself. "I must be months and *months* old by now. But how am I going to persuade my Mummy, and everybody else in the world (which consisted of the people who lived in his house, the postman, the dustmen, the vicar, and the lady-next-door whose cat he chased on Thursday mornings) to stop calling me What-a-Mess and begin calling me by my real name, Prince Amir of Kinjan?" It was indeed a huge problem.

How could he even *begin* to make people treat him as a
Prince (which his name said he was) and not as a small,
fawn, Afghan puppy of great scruffiness (which he was)?
All this thinking gave him a slight headache, so he jumped
down from his dent and went into the Special Gallop which
he had recently invented. To do this, he made his back
legs go slightly faster than his front legs, so that he galloped in
huge, backward spirals. He hit the clothes-prop and the
bird-bath but it made him feel much better.
It also did the trick. He suddenly remembered something his
mother had once said to him.

"You want to be called 'Prince', do you?" she had said.
"Well now, nobody is going to call you 'Prince' until you
start behaving like a prince. Just look at your coat for a start
– all twigs and burrs and eggshell. Princes don't look like that.
Nor do princes hide in the cupboard in terror when
the dustmen call. Princes are brave and fearless. And they
have beautifully groomed, glossy coats."

His Big Think had borne fruit at last. He now knew what to do. "Arise, Prince Amir!" he said to himself (he was sitting on a cabbage), "and prepare to start your new life as a brave, beautiful, glossy Royal Hound!"

He tackled his coat first of all. This was easy, because the man was halfway through varnishing the garden shed and What-a-Mess had heard him tell the lady that good varnish was the finest thing in the world for giving a deep, rich gloss.

What-a-Mess trotted over to the garden shed. By the door
was a brush and a large tin of varnish. He dipped a paw
into the tin and tried to flick the sticky stuff over his back,
but it went into his eye, which was painful. So he tipped the
tin onto its side, watched carefully as a huge puddle of
varnish spilled out, and then rolled himself over and over in it.

But when he stood up and took a look at the result, his coat
was not glossy at all. Well, it was a *bit* shiny, but mostly
it was wet-looking and bedraggled.
Then he remembered the man saying, "After varnishing,
remember to sand well. It's the sanding that brings up
the gloss."
The puppy went round to the back of the greenhouse where
a pile of sand was kept for potting plants.

It was such fun rolling in the sand that for a moment he forgot that he was a prince and built himself a sandcastle or two. But then he pulled himself together and inspected his coat to see how it was getting on. It gleamed a bit in the sunshine, but it still looked decidedly strange.

"Of course!" he said. "Now it needs grooming. It needs brushing and combing."

The Prince did not possess a brush or a comb,
but he reckoned that he could get much the same effect by
running at full speed through the rose-bed.

He started his run at the far end of the garden by the pool.
As he crossed the runner beans he was going well and
putting on speed all the time. He soared over the privet
hedge like a Grand National winner and was running like
the wind when he hit the roses.

His scheme partly worked. The thorns had a slight
combing effect and the leaves brushed him to a certain extent.
But as he hurtled into the roses, one prickly bush
became completely entangled in the matted fur round his
rear leg and he found it still attached to him as he made
his way into the house.

Prince-like he walked, head held proudly high, dripping
sand and varnish and dragging a complete rose-bush
behind him, into the sitting-room where the family was having tea . . .

The rest of the day was a nightmare.

Everybody shouted at him. They rushed him outside
and cut the rose-bush out of his coat with clippers.
They rubbed him with strong-smelling stuff they called
turpentine. They squirted him with detergent. They hosed
him down in the back garden. Then they rubbed him –
painfully – with a towel and put him in the boiler-house to dry out.

That night the Prince, damp, sore and miserable, decided
to run away.

"That'll show them!" he said fiercely to himself.
"When I'm gone they'll be sorry. They'll miss me when I'm not
here. Come back, little puppy, they'll cry. Come back,
little Prince! But I will be gone. For *ever!*"

It was a very dark night indeed when he nosed his way out
of the boiler-house. At first he could see by the light from
a torch, where the man was trying to get the dent out of the
roof of his car. But beyond it was pitch darkness.

The Prince had to keep reminding himself that princes are brave and fearless. His Mummy had said so.
So going into his Special Gallop, he sped forth into the black unknown.

He had no idea how far he had specially galloped –
he thought about five hundred miles – when he found himself
inside what seemed to be a cavern. A forest lair of wild beasts?
he wondered, suddenly feeling very young and rather un-brave.

Nose twitching, he moved forward cautiously. He could
not see his paw in front of his face.
Something cold and curling wrapped itself round his neck.

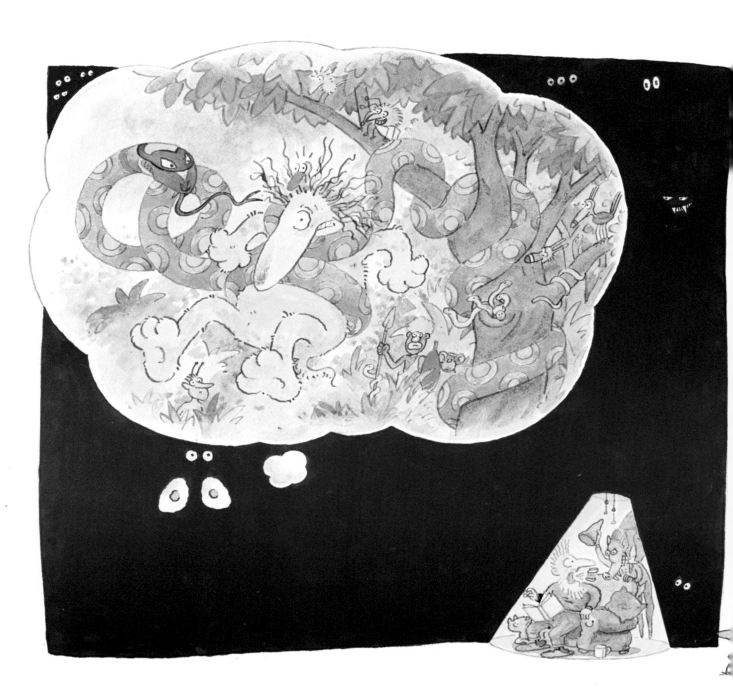

"A snake!" he yelped, springing back. But the thing
would not let go. The puppy bit it hard, but it only coiled
itself tighter. He plunged and fought and finally struggled free.

Thoroughly unhappy by now, he tried to get out of the cave, but backed straight into the jaws of something waiting behind him. As he felt teeth going for his back legs, he jumped high in the air to get away from the creature. Something was waiting up there too and it hit him a painful blow on the nose which made his eyes water.

And then he heard a great rumbling noise high overhead.
The puppy crouched low, trying to make himself as tiny as
possible in the hope that whatever it was would not notice
him. What could have made the noise? Some big, huge,
gigantic animal?

It was thunder. A summer storm had blown up and
brilliant flashes of lightning began to light up the sky.
For the first time, the Prince could see where he was.
He was not in a wild beast's lair at all. He recognised exactly
where he was. He was in the garden shed.

The first flash of lightning showed the garden hose coiled on the floor in front of him, all tangled and scratched where he had bitten it.

The second flash showed the hay-rake he had backed into, hanging on the wall, its big wooden teeth pointing towards him.

The third flash showed a string of huge, Spanish onions hanging from the ceiling above his head.

But best of all, the fourth flash showed him the house,
his home, just a few yards away across the grass.
Where his mother would be lying asleep in her basket . . .

"I think," he thought to himself as he sped across to the
house, squeezed through the cat-door and curled up beside
the dark shape of his mother, "I think I will put off being a
prince until a later date. Perhaps next Wednesday.
No, that's the day the dustmen call and I'll be in the cupboard all
day. The day after. No, I can't be a prince then.
That's the day I chase the lady-next-door's cat . . ."

His mother stirred in her basket.
"Who's that?" she murmured.

"It's only me," said the puppy, happily, "What-a-Mess!"

And exactly one and two-fifths of a second later, he was deep in blissful sleep.